CH

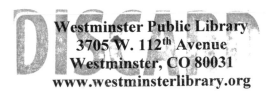

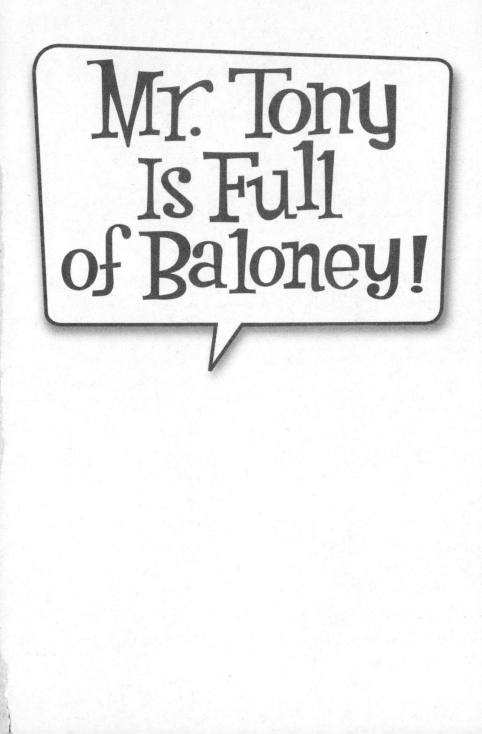

Mr. Tony Is Full of Baloney!

Dan Gutman

Pictures by
Jim Paillot

HARPER
An Imprint of HarperCollins*Publishers*

To Emma

Library of Congress Cataloging-in-Publication Data

Gutman, Dan.

    Mr. Tony is full of baloney! / Dan Gutman ; pictures by Jim Paillot. – 1st ed.

       p.   cm. – (My weird school daze ; #11)

    Summary: The After-School Kids' Kare director wants to get into The Guinness Book of World Records, and A.J. and the gang jump in to help him.

    ISBN 978-0-06-170400-0 (lib. bdg.) – ISBN 978-0-06-170399-7 (pbk.)

    [1. Schools–Fiction.   2. World records–Fiction.   3. Humorous stories.]   I. Paillot, Jim, ill.   II. Title.   III. Title: Mister Tony is full of baloney!

PZ7.G9846Mrq 2010   2010015905

[Fic]–dc22   CIP

                                                        AC

Typography by Joel Tippie

19 20   CG/LSCH   10 9 8 7 6

❖

First Edition

Contents

My Mom's Big Nose

My name is A.J. and I hate asparagus.

Ha! I bet you were thinking I was going to say I hate school. But I didn't. So nah-nah-nah boo-boo on you. That just goes to show that you shouldn't count your chickens before they're hatched.

I really don't know what that means, but

my mom is always saying you shouldn't count your chickens before they're hatched. Nobody knows why. I wouldn't want to count chickens even *after* they were hatched. Who wants to count chickens at *all*? I've heard of people counting sheep, but never chickens. I don't even know anybody who *has* chickens. Except for maybe the one we keep in the refrigerator for dinner. And it's easy to count one chicken.

One.

See? You're done counting.*

Where was I?

---

* What are you looking down here for? The story is up there, dumbhead.

Oh, yeah. You'll never believe what happened to me a couple of weeks ago. I came home from school that Thursday and my mom said, "I have big news, A.J.!"

"Your nose isn't *that* big," I replied.

"Very funny," my mom said. "The big news is that I'm going back to work."

"WHAT?!"

Before my sister and I were born, Mom had a job. She worked in a restaurant. That was back in ancient times, when dinosaurs roamed the earth. My mom stopped working so she could take care of us. That's not even like working at all because they don't give you any money for taking care of your own kids. Besides, I figure I'm so much fun to be around that taking care of me isn't even like work.

"I decided you kids are old enough now so that I can get a job again," Mom told me, "and we could use some extra money around here."

"What kind of a job?" I asked her. "Are

you going to be a jet fighter pilot or a brain surgeon?"

Having your mom as a brain surgeon would be cool. On Take Your Child to Work Day, you could watch her open up people's heads and look inside. That would be awesome!

"No," she explained. "I'm starting a little catering company called The Six Moms. I'm teaming up with Andrea's, Michael's, Ryan's, Emily's, and Neil's mothers."

"Catering?" I asked. "What's 'catering'?"

"We're going to make sandwiches and things like that for parties," Mom said.

I slapped my head.

"Sandwiches?" I said. "People can make

their *own* sandwiches. All you have to do is take a piece of bread and put stuff on it. Then you put another piece of bread on top of the stuff. Amazing! You made a sandwich!"

"We're going to make *fancy* sandwiches," my mom told me.

That made no sense, because all sandwiches go to the same place after you eat them.

"You should make something people *need*," I told her, "like a homework machine. Or something to spray on your skin so girls will stop bothering you."

"A.J., the important thing is that my new job is going to affect *you*, too," Mom told me.

"Me? What do I have to do with your job?"

"Well, I just signed you up for the after-school program," Mom said.

WHAT?!

Deal or No Deal

The after-school program?

Nooooooooooooooooooooooooooooooo!

Not the after-school program! *Anything* but the after-school program!

It's bad enough that I have to go to school for a million hundred hours during the day. Now I'd have to go to school after school is *over*!

I thought I was gonna die. This was the worst thing to happen to me since TV Turnoff Week. My life was finished.

"Can't you just poke my eyeballs out instead of sending me to the after-school program?" I asked my mom. "That would be more fun."

"The after-school program *will* be fun, A.J.!" she told me. "You'll get to play games, sing songs, make projects, and be with your friends. That's got to be better than sitting around the house watching TV after school."

"I *like* sitting around the house watching TV after school!" I told her. "What could be better than sitting around the house watching TV?"

No matter what I said, I couldn't talk her out of it. My mom was going back to work, and I had to be in the after-school program.

When I met up with my friends walking to school on Friday morning, I could tell they were all depressed.

"I guess you heard the bad news," said Michael, who never ties his shoes.

"Yeah," said Ryan, who will eat anything, even stuff that isn't food. "Starting today, we have to go to the after-school program."

"This is *horrible*," said Neil, who we

call the nude kid even though he wears clothes. "This is the worst day of my life."

"Our lives are over," I said. "Bummer in the summer."

That's when Andrea Young, this annoying girl with curly brown hair, came skipping down the street. She was with her crybaby friend Emily.

"Did you hear the news?" Andrea said, all excited. "Our moms are starting a catering business! And we're going to be in the after-school program!"

Ugh! Not only did I have to go to school after school, but I had to go to school after school with Little Miss Know-It-All *Andrea*. It was definitely the worst day in the history of the world.

I was in a bad mood all day long. I couldn't concentrate on anything my teacher, Mr. Granite, was saying. All I could think about was the after-school program.

Just before the three-o'clock bell rang,

we had to go to the all-purpose room for an assembly.* I sat next to Ryan. Little Miss Perfect sat in front of us.

Our principal, Mr. Klutz, got up on the stage. He has no hair at all. I mean *none*. They should use his head in lighthouses to send signals to ships at sea.

Mr. Klutz held up his hand and made a peace sign, which means "shut up."

"I have two announcements to make," he told us. "First, please welcome our new health teacher, Ms. Leakey."

We all clapped for some lady who got up onstage. She looked really healthy,

---

*Why is it called an assembly? We don't put anything together.

so I guess it's good that she's a health teacher.

"Second," Mr. Klutz continued, "Ella Mentry School is going to have a food drive."

"Food drive?" I whispered to Ryan. "What's up with that? Food can't drive. That would be weird to have a chicken driving your car."

"No, dumbhead," Ryan whispered back. "A food drive isn't when a chicken drives

14

your car. It's when you drive a chicken *around* in your car."

"Why would anybody want to drive a chicken around in their car?" I asked Ryan.

Andrea turned around, rolled her eyes, and said, *"Shhhhhh!"*

"A food drive is when you collect food for needy people," Mr. Klutz announced.

Oh. I knew that.

Mr. Klutz told us there are a lot of kids who don't have enough to eat.

"Hunger is a big problem in our country," he said, "so we're going to collect as much food as we can and bring it to a food bank."

"Food bank?" I whispered to Ryan. "Who puts food in a bank? Wouldn't it smell really bad after a while?"

"How would you fit the food in a bank anyway?" Ryan whispered back. "You can't push it through the little slot. Food should be put in a refrigerator."

"Mr. Klutz probably keeps his *money* in the refrigerator," I whispered. Ryan laughed.

Andrea turned around again so she could roll her eyes and shush at us. What is her problem? Why can't a bank full of food fall on her head?

"A food bank is a place that gives food to hungry people," Mr. Klutz told us.

"I knew that," I whispered to Ryan.

"And to help you kids get excited about our food drive, I'll make a deal with you," Mr. Klutz said. "If you collect 3,000 pounds of food, I'll jump out of an airplane in an ape suit and land on the roof of the school."

"WOW!" we all said, which is "MOM" upside down.

Mr. Klutz has been taking parachuting lessons ever since he went to principal camp. He loves jumping out of planes.

"3,000 pounds?" Michael called out. "That's a lot of food, Mr. Klutz. How about we collect 2,000 pounds?"

"3,000 pounds of food," Mr. Klutz repeated. "That's my final offer. Take it or leave it."

"We'll take it!" we all shouted.

It would be hilarious to see Mr. Klutz jump out of a plane in an ape suit. Not many principals are willing to do stuff like that.

Mr. Klutz is nuts.

Mr. Tony Is Weird

Brrrriiiiiiiiiinnnnnnnnnnggggggggg!!!

The three-o'clock bell rang. We watched out the window while most of the other kids got on the buses or were picked up by their parents. We were all really sad. Emily was wiping her eyes like she was about to start crying. What a crybaby!

"Look at all those kids," Neil the nude kid said, "going home to their TV sets."

"To their video games," said Michael.

"To their pets," said Andrea.

"To their snacks," said Ryan.

"And we have to stay here just because our moms want to make some dumb sandwiches," I said. "It's not fair."

We had to walk a million hundred miles all the way to the other side of the school, where the ASKK room is. ASKK stands for "After-School Kids' Kare," which makes no sense at all because "care" is spelled with a *C*, not a *K*. How are we supposed to learn how to spell if they can't even spell "ASKK" right?

The grown-up in charge of ASKK is Mr. Tony, but he wasn't there yet. The door was locked. Some other kids were waiting in the hall. I guess their moms had to make sandwiches, too.

"I have an idea," I told the guys. "Let's make a run for it!"

"They probably have guards with

machine guns who will shoot us if we try to escape," said Ryan.

"Maybe we can dig a tunnel and escape to freedom," said Michael. "I saw that in a war movie once. The prisoners dug a hole in the ground and hid the dirt down their pants so the guards wouldn't notice."

"I'm not putting dirt down my pants," I said.

"We don't have a shovel anyway," said Neil. "We can't dig a tunnel."

"Boys!" Andrea said, rolling her eyes.

That's when the strangest thing in the history of the world happened. A guy came over.

Well, that's not the strange part because

guys come over all the time. The strange part was that the guy came over on a pogo stick, and he was juggling three balls.

"Mr. Tony, reporting for duty!" he said.

We all giggled because Mr. Tony said "duty," which sounds just like "doody." It's okay to say "*D-U-T-Y*," but grown-ups get really mad when you say "*D-O-O-D-Y*." Nobody knows why.

Mr. Tony jumped off the pogo stick. He's a big guy with a mustache. He saluted us like he was in the army. I saw he had a big white Band-Aid on his arm.

"Ten-hut!" he said.

Army guys always say "Ten-hut" when they want you to stand up straight.

Nobody knows why.

"At ease," Mr. Tony said. He handed out name tags to each of us and opened the door to the ASKK room. "I won't tolerate any foolishness in here. I run a tight ship."

I looked around the ASKK room. There wasn't any ship in there. I don't understand why people are always talking about ships. What's up with that?

"Are we going boating?" I asked.

"Of course not!" Mr. Tony yelled. "What would make you think we'd go boating in the after-school program?"

"How should I know?" I asked. "You're the one who brought it up."

Mr. Tony is weird.

Pizza and Pogo-Juggling

Mr. Tony seemed like he was really mean. But suddenly, he broke out into a big grin.

"I was just kidding with that army stuff," he said. "Welcome to the ASKK program! Are you kids ready to have fun?"

"Yes!" said all the girls.

"No," said all the boys.

"Before we have fun," Andrea said, "may I ask you a question, Mr. Tony?"

"Certainly," he replied.

"Why were you juggling on a pogo stick?"

"I'm trying to get into *The Guinness Book of World Records*," Mr. Tony said. "The record for pogo-juggling is almost 25 minutes. I want to break it."

Pogo-juggling? Now I *knew* Mr. Tony was weird.

"Did you get hurt pogo-juggling?" asked Emily. "Is that why you have a Band-Aid on your arm?"

"It's not a Band-Aid. It's a nicotine

patch," Mr. Tony explained. "I'm trying to quit smoking."

"Cigarettes are really bad for you," said Ryan.

"I know," Mr. Tony said. "I used to be a chain-smoker."

"You smoked chains?" I asked. "That's weird."

"A chain-smoker is somebody who smokes all the time, Arlo!" Andrea said. She calls me by my real name because she knows I don't like it.

"I knew that," I lied.

"My doctor says that if I do a lot of exercise, it will help me quit smoking," Mr. Tony said. "So I thought I would try to do something active and get into *The Guinness Book of World Records*. If I was the best in the world at something, I think I would have the confidence to stop smoking."

That made sense, I guess.

Mr. Tony took us on a tour of the ASKK room.

"On nice days you can play out in the playground," he told us, "but there are lots of fun things to do in here too."

The ASKK room was divided into a bunch of little stations. There was one station for drawing pictures, one station for arts and crafts, one station for cooking, one station for making stuff with beads and Legos, and one station for playing board games.*

"You can do whatever you want," said Mr. Tony. "You can even do your

---

* Board games are boring. That's why they're called bored games.

homework if you'd like, over here in the homework station."

That's where Andrea will probably spend her time. She *loves* homework. I bet that on her birthday she asks her parents to give her more homework.

"I don't want to do any of that stuff," I told Mr. Tony.

"Me neither," said Ryan.

"We don't want to be here," said Michael.

"Yeah, we want to go home," said Neil the nude kid.

Mr. Tony looked sad for a minute. But then he snapped his fingers.

"I have an idea for something you boys

would like to do!" he said. "Let's make a pizza!"

Pizza? I *love* pizza! I could eat pizza all day long. Well, maybe not in the shower. That would be weird.

"We don't know how to make a pizza," said Ryan.

"I'll show you how!" Mr. Tony said. "It's easy."

He told us he was born in Italy, and his father has been making pizza for fifty years.

"Doesn't your father get tired?" I asked. Nobody laughed even though I said something funny.

Mr. Tony showed us how to throw the

pizza dough up in the air. We all got to
help spread the sauce and the cheese on
top of it. Then we put the pizza in the oven
for like a million hundred minutes. When
it was done, each of us got a slice.

The pizza was great! In fact, it was more than great. It was the most awesome pizza in the history of the world, because we helped make it.

Maybe going to the after-school program won't be so horrible after all.

The Sequel to Halloween

It was getting dark outside when my mom finally came to pick me up from school.

"So, tell me all about the after-school program," she said as we got into the car. "What did you do?"

"Nothin'," I said.

Any time your mom asks what you did

during the day, always say "Nothin'." Even if an alien spaceship landed in the middle of the lunchroom that day, just tell your mom that nothing happened. Even if a spaceship landed and a bunch of alien Elvis impersonators got out and sang "Hound Dog," just say "Nothin'." That's the first rule of being a kid.

"Did you and The Six Moms make a lot of sandwiches today?" I asked her.

"No, we don't have any customers yet," Mom told me. "Our company is just getting off the ground."

I told her that it will be hard to make sandwiches if her company is floating around in the air.

We emptied out my backpack, and there was a sheet of paper inside telling the parents all about the Ella Mentry School food drive. So my mom called Ryan's, Michael's, and Neil's moms and arranged for me and my friends to go out collecting food together.

The next day was Saturday, and me and the guys met up at Michael's house. Our moms gave us pillowcases to hold the food we collected. Then we went door-to-door around the neighborhood asking for food.

"We're collecting food for hungry people," we said at the first house we visited.

The lady gave us a can of tomato sauce.

"We're collecting food for hungry

people," we said at the next house.

A man gave us a can of beans.

We went to a bunch of houses, and everybody was happy to give us some food. The pillowcases were starting to get heavy.

When we came to the next house, you'll never believe in a million hundred years who answered the door.

Nobody. You can't answer doors, because doors don't talk. But you'll never believe who *opened* the door.

It was Mr. Klutz!

"Ah!" he said. "I see you boys are collecting food for the food drive. Good work! Here's a can of soup."

"Thanks, Mr. Klutz!" we said.

"Remember, if you kids collect 3,000 pounds of food, I'll jump out of a plane in an ape suit and land on the roof of the school."

"How will you be able to see the roof

of the school from the sky?" Michael asked.

"There's a big red circle on the roof," Mr. Klutz told us. "I should be able to land right on it unless there's a lot of wind that day."

Before we left, Mr. Klutz gave all of us cookies. We ate them as we walked down the street.

"Y'know," Ryan said as we ate our cookies, "this is almost like Halloween! We just knocked on Mr. Klutz's door, and he gave us treats."

That's when I came up with the greatest idea in the history of the world. When Ryan knocked on the next door and a lady opened it, I held out my pillowcase and yelled, "Trick or treat!"

"Isn't Halloween in October?" the lady asked. "That was months ago."

I didn't know what to say. I didn't know what to do. I had to think fast.

"You know how really good movies have sequels?" I said. "Well, they decided that really good holidays should have sequels, too. Today is the sequel to Halloween."

"The sequel to Halloween?" the lady said. "Hmmm, I never heard of that."

"Oh, it was in all the newspapers," I told her.

"But you boys aren't even wearing costumes," she said.

"Oh, costumes aren't allowed on the sequel to Halloween," I told her. "Everybody knows that."

"Well . . . okay," the lady said. "Let me see if I have any candy."

She came back a minute later with four Hershey bars.

"Thanks!" we all said. "Happy Halloween!"

What a scam!

As we walked down the street eating our Hershey bars, the guys all told me I was a genius for coming up with the sequel to Halloween.

We stopped off at a few more houses, yelled "Trick or treat!" at each one, and told the people all about the sequel to Halloween. I got a Crunch bar, some M&M'S, and a Reese's Peanut Butter Cup. By the time I got home, I was sick to my stomach. I thought I was gonna throw up.

It was the greatest day of my life.

Food drives are cool.

The Land of No Toilets

When I got to school on Monday morning, everybody was putting cans of food into big cardboard boxes by the front office. The kids at our school collected a *lot* of food.

And you'll never believe in a million hundred years what happened at school that day.

Nothing.

No, really! I mean it. I'm not just saying that. Nothing happened. It was the most boring day in the history of the world.

But at the *end* of the day, I went to the ASKK room with the guys. A few minutes later Mr. Tony showed up. He wasn't jumping on a pogo stick and juggling this time. He was jogging with a spoon in his mouth, and there was an egg on the spoon.

"Mr. Tony reporting for duty!" he said after he took the spoon out of his mouth. We all giggled because he said "duty" again.

"Mr. Tony, why were you holding a spoon in your mouth with an egg on it?"

Andrea asked.

"I'm trying
to get into
*The Guinness
Book of World
Records* for
egg-jogging,"
Mr. Tony
told us. "The
record for
running a
mile while
holding a spoon

in your mouth with an egg on it is over
eight minutes. I'm trying to break it."

"And that's going to help you quit

smoking?" Andrea asked.

"Yes!" Mr. Tony said. "As long as I have a spoon in my mouth, I can't smoke."

Mr. Tony sure comes up with weird ways to quit smoking.

"Hey, how about we play a word game today?" he said. "Who can use the word 'spaghetti' in a sentence?"

Andrea got all excited and was waving her arm in the air like it was on fire. But Mr. Tony called on me. So nah-nah-nah boo-boo on Andrea.

"Abraham Lincoln gave the Spaghettisburg Address," I said.

Everybody laughed even though I didn't say anything funny.

"Lincoln gave the *Gettysburg* address, Arlo!" Little Miss Perfect said, rolling her eyes. "Not Spaghettisburg!"

"Oh, snap!" said Ryan.

"Try another one, A.J.," Mr. Tony said. "Can you use the word 'toiletries' in a sentence?"

"Sure," I said. "Out in the forest there were some oak trees, some maple trees, and some toilet trees."

Everybody laughed again even though I didn't say anything funny.

"There's no such thing as a toilet tree, Arlo!" Andrea said, rolling her eyes again.

"Yeah, toilets don't grow on trees," said Emily. "Toiletries are what you bring in a

little bag when you go on vacation."

"Oh, yeah?" I said. "Why would you take a toilet with you on vacation? Where do you go on vacation anyway? The Land of No Toilets? When I go on vacation, they have toilets there *already*. I don't have to bring one with me."

"Oh, snap!" said Ryan.

I was just yanking her chain, but Emily looked like she was going to cry, as usual. Sheesh, get a grip! That girl needs to go to the drugstore and buy a chill pill. She'll cry at the drop of a hat.

Actually, it's true. One time after school I took Emily's hat and dropped it in a puddle. She started crying, of course.

"No arguing in the ASKK room," said Mr. Tony. "I have an idea! Let's play Simon Says!"

"I hate Simon Says," I said.

"Well, we're going to play Simon Says, A.J., and I want *you* to be Simon," said Mr. Tony. "We will do anything you tell us to do as long as you say 'Simon Says' first."

"Anything?" I asked.

"Anything," Mr. Tony said.

"Anything?" I repeated.

"Anything," Mr. Tony repeated.

We went back and forth like that for a while.

"Okay," I said. "Simon Says we stop playing Simon Says and make a pizza instead."

"Yeah!" everybody shouted. "Pizza! Pizza! Pizza!"

"Okay! Okay!" Mr. Tony said. "You win. And because you kids are so smart, we'll make *two* pizzas today."

"Yay!"

We made pizza just like last time, but Mr. Tony gave us some mushrooms, sausage, and bacon to put on one of them. He says you can put anything on a pizza.

While we ate, we asked Mr. Tony about pogo-juggling and egg-jogging. He said he hadn't broken any records yet, but he was working on it. His goals were to get into *The Guinness Book of World Records* someday and to stop smoking.

"Wouldn't it be great to be the best person in the world at something?" he asked us.

"That would be cool," I agreed.

Mr. Tony told us that you didn't have to be a great singer or athlete or superstar to break a world record. Regular people can break records, too.

"A man in England smashed forty eggs against his head in a minute," he told us. "He's in *The Guinness Book of World Records* for that."

"WOW!" we all said, which is "MOM" upside down.

"And there's this man in New York who pushed an orange for a mile with his nose in 22 minutes and 41 seconds."

Mr. Tony told us more stories about

crazy people who were in *The Guinness Book of World Records*. There was a guy in Australia who put on twenty pairs of underpants in one minute to set the world record for putting on underpants in one minute. Can you believe that? And some other guy smashed forty-six wooden toilet seat lids with his head. And then somebody in Texas got into a bathtub with eighty-seven rattlesnakes to set a world record. It was hilarious.

If you ask me, people who try to set records are weird.

My Genius Idea

My mom told me that her catering company wasn't doing very well. The Six
Moms still didn't have any customers,
and nobody wanted to buy their fancy
sandwiches. Mom said it was because of
the economy, whatever that means.

But the food drive at school was going

great. Every morning there was more food in the cardboard boxes by the front office. And then, finally, one morning we saw a big sign on the wall . . .

WE DID IT! WE COLLECTED 3,000 POUNDS OF FOOD! GREAT JOB, ELLA MENTRY SCHOOL STUDENTS!

At lunchtime I sat in the vomitorium with the guys. Andrea and her girlie friends sat at the next table so they could annoy us. Me and Michael had peanut butter and jelly sandwiches (that weren't fancy at all). Ryan and Neil the nude kid bought the school lunch. Ugh, disgusting!

"When is Mr. Klutz going to jump out of a plane in an ape suit?" asked Neil the nude kid.

"I hope he does it when we're at ASKK," said Michael.

"Hey, do you think Mr. Tony will pogo-juggle or egg-jog today?" asked Ryan.

"Who knows?" said Neil. "He sure is a weird guy."

"Maybe Mr. Tony isn't really the ASKK director at all," I told the guys. "Did you ever think of that?"

"What do you mean, A.J.?" asked Michael.

"Well, maybe Mr. Tony is an evil genius who wants to take over the world," I said. "Maybe he kidnapped our *real* ASKK director and has him tied up to some railroad tracks. Stuff like that happens all the time, you know."

At the next table, Andrea looked all worried.

"What's the matter?" I asked her. "Are you afraid that our real ASKK director is tied to the railroad tracks?"

"No, Arlo," Andrea said. "I'm worried about Mr. Tony."

"What about him?" I asked.

"My mother is a psychologist," she said. "She told me that some people are so desperate to be famous that they'll do just about anything to draw attention to themselves and make people like them. Like those parents who said their son was up in a hot-air balloon last year. And those two people who crashed a party at the White House."

"You think Mr. Tony is crazy?" I asked.

"No," Andrea said. "But it's sad that he thinks he has to do such crazy things so people will like him. My mom thinks that's why he's addicted to cigarettes, too."

"I know how to solve this problem," I said.

"How?" asked Emily.

"It's simple," I told them. "We just need

to make Mr. Tony famous."

"And how are we going to do that, Arlo?" Andrea asked.

We all thought and thought and thought for a million hundred seconds. That's when I came up with the greatest idea in the history of the world. It was like a lightbulb appeared over my head.*

"Mr. Tony is great at making pizza, right?" I asked.

"Right," everybody replied.

"Well," I said, "what if he made the biggest pizza in the world? That would make him famous. Maybe he would get into *The*

---

* How did people come up with any ideas before the lightbulb was invented? Maybe candles appeared over their heads.

Guinness Book of World Records. And if your mom is right, maybe Mr. Tony would stop smoking, too."

"That just might work, Arlo!" Andrea said.

"A.J., you're a genius!" said Michael.

I should get the No Bell Prize for that idea.

That's a prize they give out to people who don't have bells.

The Biggest Pizza in the World

Instead of going out for recess, we all rushed over to the school library. Our media specialist, Mrs. Roopy, was in there eating her lunch.

"To what do I owe the pleasure of your company?" she asked.

That's grown-up talk for "What are

you doing here?"

"We need to see *The Guinness Book of World Records* right away!" I told her. I was all out of breath.

Mrs. Roopy put her hand on my forehead.

"A.J., are you feeling okay?" she asked. "I've never heard you say you wanted to read a book before. Maybe I should call an ambulance and get you to the hospital."

"He's fine," said Neil the nude kid.

"We need to do some research, Mrs. Roopy," said Andrea. "We want to find out how big the biggest pizza in the world is."

Mrs. Roopy got *The Guinness Book of World Records* off a shelf, and we all

gathered around her to look at it.

"Let's see," she said, leafing through the book. "Here's a man who balanced a refrigerator on his teeth for ten seconds. That's remarkable! And here's a man who ate a whole bicycle. That's amazing!"

"Nothing about giant pizzas in there?" asked Ryan.

Finally Mrs. Roopy found the section on food, and there it was: the biggest pizza in the world was made in South Africa in 1990. It was 386 feet around, and it had 1,764 pounds of cheese and 1,985 pounds of tomato sauce on it.

"WOW!" Michael said, which is "MOM" upside down. "That's a big pizza!"

"How could we possibly make a pizza bigger than that one?" asked Ryan.

That's when I came up with the greatest idea in the history of the world.

"Our school collected over 3,000 pounds of food," I said. "We could use the food from the food drive to make our pizza!"

"The food we collected is for hungry people, A.J.," Mrs. Roopy said. "It would be wrong to use that food just to break a world record."

"Nobody puts beans or soup on pizza anyway," said Ryan.

Okay, so maybe my idea wasn't so great after all.

We all thought and thought and thought. I thought so hard that I thought my head was going to explode. Suddenly, Andrea got this gleam in her eye.

"I know!" she said. "The Six Moms can supply the ingredients for our pizza! Our school could be the first customer of our moms' new catering company!"

"Yeah!" said Emily, who always agrees with everything Andrea says.

It was a good idea, I had to admit. But there wasn't any lightbulb over Andrea's head, and I wasn't about to admit out loud that she had a good idea.

"That's the dumbest idea in the history of the world," I said.

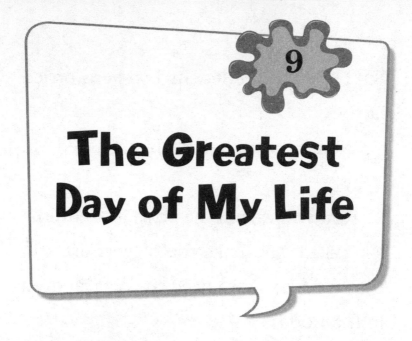

The Greatest
Day of My Life

"I love it!" Mr. Tony said when we told him about our idea. "Why didn't *I* think of making the biggest pizza in the world? That will be a lot easier than pogo-juggling and egg-jogging!"

Everybody was excited about getting into *The Guinness Book of World Records*.

But Little Miss Perfect had on her worried face.

"What's the matter, Andrea?" asked Mr. Tony.

"How will we put the pizza in an oven?" she asked. "To make the biggest pizza in the world, don't we need the biggest oven in the world?"

"Andrea's right!" said Emily, who always thinks Andrea is right.

"No problem," said Mr. Tony. "I'll take care of that. We'll heat up the tomato sauce and cheese first and then spread them on the pizza crust. We'll have to make the pizza out in the playground, because it will be too big to fit in here."

"But there's another problem," Andrea said. "What will we do with the pizza after we make it? We can't eat a pizza that big. And it would be terrible to throw it away, especially after our food drive. What a waste of food."

"I know! We can give the pizza to a food bank so they can feed hungry people!" I suggested.

"A.J., you're a genius!" Michael said.

No wonder I'm in the gifted and talented program.

Everything was falling into place. Mom said that The Six Moms would be happy to supply the ingredients for our giant pizza. Ms. LaGrange, our lunch lady, said she would help us heat up the sauce in the kitchen and put the pizza together. Mr. Tony called *The Guinness Book of World Records* people, and they said they would send someone over to see our pizza in person and prove it was the biggest one in the world.

"Let's not tell anyone else about our giant pizza," Mr. Tony told us. "Not even Mr. Klutz. If the word gets out that we're making the biggest pizza in the world, somebody might try to steal our idea and make a bigger pizza than ours."

My lips were sealed. But not with glue or anything. That would be weird.

* * *

Finally, the day came to put together our giant pizza. During recess, three huge trucks drove up onto the playground. One had a ton of cheese in it. One had a ton of tomato sauce in it. And one had a huge pizza crust. Guys wearing overalls got out of the trucks and started unloading all the stuff.

"How did The Six Moms get a truck full of tomato sauce?" I asked my mom.

"We went to Rent-A-Truck-Full-of-Tomato-Sauce," she said. "You can rent anything."

Everybody pitched in to help. Ms. Hannah, our art teacher, put gigantic pieces of cardboard down on the playground. We all unrolled the giant pizza crust onto the cardboard. It was the size of a swimming pool!

Then Mr. Tony came out of the school. He was carrying this thing that looked like a big Super Soaker. There was a tank strapped to his back, like the kind scuba divers wear.

"What's that thing?" Ryan asked.

"It's a flamethrower," said Mr. Tony.

"What does it do?" asked Michael.

"It throws flame," said Mr. Tony.

"So it has the perfect name," I said.

Mr. Tony pulled the trigger on the flamethrower, and a giant explosion of fire came flying out! We all jumped back. I could feel the heat on my face. Mr. Tony walked around the pizza crust, shooting fire all over it.

"That thing is *cool*!" we all said.

"Where did you get a flamethrower?"
Neil the nude kid asked Mr. Tony.

"From Rent-A-Flamethrower," he replied.
"You can rent anything."

After a few minutes of flamethrowing,
the giant pizza crust had turned from
white to brown.

"Okay," Mr. Tony said as he turned off the flamethrower. "It's cooked. Pour on the sauce!"

The truck full of tomato sauce backed up to the pizza and dumped its load onto the crust. The Six Moms used rakes and shovels to spread the sauce evenly.

"Bring on the cheese!" shouted Mr. Tony.

The Six Moms shoveled cheese off the truck and carried it over to the pizza.

"This is so exciting!" Ryan's mom said as she scattered shovelfuls of cheese on top of the sauce. "Our first catering job!"

"What a way to start our new company!" said Michael's mom.

"This is much more fun than making little sandwiches!" said Emily's mom.

"And now for the toppings!" my mom said, taking a bucket out of her car. "Pepperoni...salami...baloney...pastrami..."

"Mom," I complained, "pizza doesn't have lunch meat on it!"

"It's a *fancy* pizza," Mom told me as she flung the slices of meat on top like little Frisbees.

"Go ahead," Mr. Tony said. "You can put *anything* on a pizza."

Finally, after a million hundred hours, the pizza was finished. We all stepped back to look at our masterpiece. We did it! We made the biggest pizza in the world.

Everybody in school came out into the playground to see what all the excitement was about. The teachers were taking pictures with cell phone cameras.

"I'm going to put this up on the school website!" said Mrs. Yonkers,

our computer teacher.

"I'm going to write a children's book about it!" said Mr. Macky, our reading specialist.

"What a mess I will have to clean up!" said Miss Lazar, our custodian.

"Where's Mr. Klutz?" asked Andrea. "He should be here to see this."

"Mr. Klutz told me he had to go to a meeting," said Mrs. Patty, the school secretary. "He'll be back soon."

Mr. Tony's cell phone rang. He answered it and spoke to somebody.

"It was a guy from *The Guinness Book of World Records*," he told us excitedly after he hung up. "A lady will be here in a few minutes to measure our pizza and prove we broke the record. She came all the way from England!"

"Channel 7 News called, too," Mrs. Patty said. "They're coming over to cover the story. Our pizza is going to be on TV!"

Everybody was freaking out with excitement! Mr. Tony was going to be famous, and it was all because of my genius idea. It was the greatest day of my life.

That's when the weirdest thing in the history of the world happened.

But I'm not going to tell you what it was.

Okay, okay, I'll tell you.

But you have to read the next chapter. So nah-nah-nah boo-boo on you.

Pizza Toppings

"The lady from *The Guinness Book of World Records* is here!" Mrs. Patty announced over the loudspeaker. "And so is Channel 7 News!"

Everybody was even more excited when two vans pulled up to the school driveway. The Channel 7 News team got out with cameras and microphones and stuff. We all ran over to greet the lady from *The Guinness Book of World Records*.

"Chip chip cheerio, old chap,"* she said as she shook hands with Mr. Tony. "So where is this extremely large pizza I heard so much about?"

"Follow me," Mr. Tony said.

"I can't wait to see it," said the Guinness lady. "I have seen some pretty big pizzas in my time, but—"

She never got the chance to finish her sentence because suddenly there was a loud rumbling sound over the playground.

---

* British people always say "Chip chip cheerio." Nobody knows why.

"What's that?" Andrea asked.

"Look, up in the air!" yelled Ryan.

"It's a bird!" yelled Michael.

"It's a plane!" yelled Neil the nude kid.

"No, it's a parachuting ape!" I yelled.

It was true. High above our heads, an ape was floating down over the school under a big white parachute. The Channel 7 News team pointed their cameras up in the air.

"It's not an ape," yelled Andrea. "It's Mr. Klutz in an ape suit!"

Andrea was right! And he was coming down directly over our heads! Everybody was yelling, screaming, freaking out, and waving their arms trying to signal Mr. Klutz.

"No! Not here!" we were yelling. "Not here!"

Mr. Klutz was coming down right over the pizza!

"Run for your lives!" shouted Neil the nude kid.

"Watch out!"

"Noooooooooooooooooooooooooooooo!"

That's when Mr. Klutz hit the ground, right in the middle of our pizza.

Splllllllllllaaaaaaaaaaaattttttttttt.

It was a real Kodak moment. Everybody came running over to the edge of the pizza.

"Glub glub!" Mr. Klutz yelled. "Help! I can't swim!"

"He's drowning in tomato sauce!" Emily shouted. "We've got to *do* something!"

"I'll save you!" shouted Mr. Tony. He dived headfirst into the middle of the pizza.

Mr. Klutz was flailing all over the place

like a fish on the bottom of a boat. Mr.
Tony kept trying to grab him, but they
were both covered with tomato sauce,
and they were just slipping and sliding all
over the pizza.

You should have been there! Mr. Klutz

was freaking out. We saw it live and in person. He had cheese all over his bald head. And Mr. Tony was full of baloney!

"I say, old chaps," said the Guinness lady, "why are those blokes wrestling in your giant pizza?"

"The guy with the mustache is our after-school program director," I told her, "and the bald guy with cheese on his head is our principal."

"Ah, I see," said the Guinness lady. "Pizza-wrestling must be some sort of strange American tradition, like baseball."

Finally, Mr. Tony was able to pull Mr. Klutz off the pizza. The two of them were a mess.

"Who put that giant pizza in the middle of the playground?" asked Mr. Klutz as he wiped tomato sauce off his face.

"We did," Mr. Tony told him. "We made it so we could get into *The Guinness Book of World Records*. Why did you land on our pizza?"

"It was windy," Mr. Klutz said. "I saw the big red circle down below me. I got confused. I thought it was the circle on the roof of the school. From up in the air, it looked like a target."

"It's not a target!" Mr. Tony explained. "It's the biggest pizza in the world!"

"Uh, don't count your chickens until they are hatched," said the Guinness lady.

"I'm terribly sorry, chaps, but I cannot accept this record for *The Guinness Book*."

"Why not?" we all asked.

"The rules state very clearly that people are supposed to *make* the pizza," she said, "not wrestle in it."

"Can't we get into *The Guinness Book of World Records* for making the biggest pizza with two guys wrestling in it?" asked Michael. "That must be a world record."

"Sorry, no," said the Guinness lady.

"Doesn't Mr. Klutz count as a pizza topping?" I suggested.

"I'm sorry," said the Guinness lady. "Well, thank you. I've had a lovely time, but I've got to get back to jolly old England now.

Chip chip cheerio, chaps!"

The Guinness lady left, and the Channel 7 News crew packed up their cameras and microphones.

Everybody at school was really sad. Our pizza wasn't going to be in *The Guinness Book of World Records*. Mr. Tony wasn't going to be famous. We wouldn't even be able to give our pizza to the food bank. Hungry people don't want to eat a pizza that two guys were wrestling in.*

Mr. Tony was really mad that his pizza was ruined. Mr. Klutz was really mad that his parachute jump was ruined. Miss

---

* But Ryan would. He'll eat anything, even stuff that isn't food.

Lazar was really mad because there was even more cleaning up to do, and she made us all pitch in to help out. It took a million hundred hours.

Finally, I got into the car with my mom to go home. We both smelled like pizza.

"I was *sure* we were going to get into *The Guinness Book of World Records,*" I told her.

"You shouldn't count your chickens before they're hatched," she replied.

What do chickens have to do with it? We didn't even put any chicken on the pizza.

A Happy Ending

When we got home, the phone was ring-ing. My mom picked it up. She talked with somebody for a long time.

When she hung up, she said, "I just got some more bad news, A.J."

"Your nose isn't that bad," I told her.

"Mr. Klutz is very angry about what

happened," she told me. "He says he's not going to pay us for all that tomato sauce, cheese, and crust The Six Moms bought to make the pizza."

"So?" I said.

"So my company is bankrupt," Mom told me sadly. "The Six Moms is out of business."

"Wait a minute," I said. "If The Six Moms is out of business, that means . . ."

"It means I have to take you out of the after-school program," she told me.

"Hooray!" I yelled. "I can watch TV again! Yippee!"

I was running around and jumping and going crazy. It was the greatest moment of my life.

I ran to the TV like I was in the Olympics. It had been so long since I watched TV that I almost forgot which remote control turned it on. Finally, I got the TV working.

There was a man and a lady on the screen. Below their faces it said BREAKING NEWS! I turned up the volume.

"This just in," the news lady said. "A crazy man in an ape costume jumped out of an airplane today over Ella Mentry School. He landed in an enormous pizza that was in the playground. It turns out the man was Mr. Klutz, the principal of the school. Can you believe anybody would do such a crazy thing?"

"I guess this Mr. Klutz is nuts!" said the newsman sitting next to her. "He's just another pathetic person trying to get famous. Like that guy who said his son was in a hot-air balloon. It's just so sad

that people want to be famous so badly."

"This story has a happy ending though," the news lady said. "The crazy principal was rescued by Mr. Tony, the after-school program director of Ella Mentry School. He dived right into the pizza and pulled Mr. Klutz out before that nutty principal drowned in tomato sauce."

"Mr. Tony is a *real* hero," the newsman said, "like that pilot who landed the plane on the river in New York City. Mr. Tony is the one who deserves to be famous, not that crazy principal."

"In fact," the news lady said, "we understand that Mr. Tony will be writing a book about his life story that will be made into a movie. So I guess he will be famous when this is all over."

Well, that's pretty much what happened. Maybe I'll start liking asparagus. Maybe me and the guys will count some chickens before they hatch. Maybe my mom will get a new job as a brain surgeon.

Maybe somebody will invent a homework machine. Maybe Mr. Klutz will grow some hair on his head. Maybe we'll tunnel out of the school. Maybe pogo-juggling, egg-jogging, and pizza-wrestling will become Olympic sports. Maybe Mr. Tony will stop smoking chains. Maybe we'll figure out why army guys say "Ten-hut." Maybe Mr. Tony will take us boating. Maybe the sequel to Halloween will become a real holiday. Maybe Mr. Tony will break some other record to get into *The Guinness Book of World Records*.

But it won't be easy!